Lulu Bell and the

Arabian Nights

A Random House book
Published by Random House Australia Pty Ltd
Level 3, 100 Pacific Highway, North Sydney NSW 2060
www.randomhouse.com.au

Penguin
Random House
RANDOM HOUSE BOOKS

First published by Random House Australia in 2015
Copyright © Belinda Murrell 2015
Illustrations copyright © Serena Geddes 2015

The moral right of the author and illustrator has been asserted.

Addresses for companies within the Random House Group can be found at global.penguinrandomhouse.com

National Library of Australia
Cataloguing-in-Publication Entry

Author: Murrell, Belinda
Title: Lulu Bell and the Arabian nights/Belinda Murrell; illustrated by Serena Geddes
ISBN: 978 0 85798 558 3 (paperback)
Series: Murrell, Belinda. Lulu Bell; 11
Target audience: For primary school age
Subjects: Harmony Day (Australia) – Juvenile fiction
       Multiculturalism – Juvenile fiction
Other authors/contributors: Geddes, Serena
Dewey number: A823.4

Cover and internal illustrations by Serena Geddes
Cover design by Christabella Designs
Internal design and typesetting in 16/22 pt Bembo by Ingo Voss, Voss Designs, based on series design by Anna Warren, Warren Ventures
Printed in Australia by Griffin Press, an accredited ISO AS/NZS 14001:2004 Environmental Management System printer

Random House Australia uses papers that are natural, renewable and recyclable products and made from wood grown in sustainable forests. The logging and manufacturing processes are expected to conform to the environmental regulations of the country of origin.

Lulu Bell and the Arabian Nights

Belinda Murrell

Illustrated by Serena Geddes

RANDOM HOUSE AUSTRALIA

Lulu   Dad

Mum   Gus   Rosie

To the many gorgeous parents who've helped cook up
Harmony Day feasts for our kids, especially Millie,
Barb, Mel, Sarah and Kyles – thanks for being my pals.

Chapter 1

Sword Fights

 It was a drizzly kind of day. It was after school on a Monday and a perfect afternoon for making play swords. Lulu and Rosie Bell were working with their grandfather down in the garage. Gumpa had on a pair of protective goggles. He was using an electric saw to shape a piece of wood. Dust flew up from the whirring saw as it chewed through the timber.

Gumpa had cut out two flat wooden blades. They were slightly curved like Arabian scimitars. He shaped the bottom end of the blade into a rounded handle, the hilt. The top end was shaped into a blunt point.

Lulu hammered a nail to fasten a bar across the blade to make the guard. Rosie was using sandpaper to smooth the wood on one sword. Gumpa kept an eye on their progress.

It was hard work. Sawdust drifted from the bench to the floor. Lulu had to concentrate to make sure she hit the nail straight.

'Good work, girls,' said Gumpa. He tested the guard to make sure it was firmly attached. 'They're just about finished.'

Lulu used the sandpaper to smooth the hilt of her sword. Gumpa ran his finger along the blade to make sure it was blunt. He held the sword up in front of his face in a salute.

'Here you go,' said Gumpa. 'What do you think?'

'Great! Thanks, Gumpa,' said Lulu. 'They're just what we needed for our game.'

Gumpa handed her the sword. Lulu weighed it in her hand. It felt strong. Lulu used both hands to swing the sword. She swung it over her head, around, down and up again to make a perfect figure-eight shape in the air.

Lulu grinned at Rosie. Both of the girls were wearing green velvet cloaks. 'A perfect sword for battling ghouls.'

'And *evil* wizards,' added Rosie.

'And at least forty bandits,' said Lulu.

Mum had been reading them a collection of Persian folktales called *One Thousand and One Nights*. Most people knew the stories as *The Arabian Nights*.

Lulu, Rosie and their little brother Gus had been playing games based on some of the old stories. They especially liked 'Ali Baba and the Forty Thieves', 'Aladdin's Wonderful Lamp' and 'The Ebony Horse'.

'Well, I hope we don't have too many ghouls around here,' joked Gumpa. 'I don't need any frights.'

'Let's go and show Gus,' said Rosie. She hurtled out the door.

Gumpa started to sweep up the sawdust.

'I'll help you pack up,' said Lulu. She hung the hammer back on the wall and put the sandpaper in the toolbox.

'That's okay, Lulu,' said Gumpa.
'I'll finish tidying up. You go and practise
with that sword.'

Lulu raced out into the garden.
The rain had stopped and Rosie and
Gus were zooming around in circles.
The two dogs ran with them.

Gus was wearing the new knight
costume that Mum had made him for
Christmas. The tunic was made of shiny
silver material. A lion rearing up on
its hind legs was drawn on the front.
Underneath he wore grey leggings and
a long-sleeved T-shirt. He had a red
sash tied around his waist. On his head
was a helmet made from an ice-cream
container covered in silver foil.

The three children had been playing
sword fights since the summer holidays.
At first they had made flimsy swords from

bamboo. Then Gumpa had promised to make them some proper wooden play swords. Lulu loved her new toy.

Gus already had a sword from Gumpa. He waved it in the air.

'On guard!' yelled Gus.

Lulu ran to meet the challenge. Her cloak swirled around her shoulders. Loud clangs rang though the air as Lulu and Gus fought with their swords. Lulu danced back and forth. Every few minutes she would spring into a cartwheel then lunge back to hit Gus's sword.

'Got you,' cried Lulu, as her sword clashed against Gus's. Gus tumbled into a forward roll.

'My turn,' called Rosie. Gus wheeled away. Rosie swooped in to take his place, with a loud, 'Take that!'

The two dogs sat and watched. They knew not to get in the way. Jessie smiled her big doggy smile.

Rosie spun around in a circle then dashed forward to attack. Lulu sprang into another cartwheel to escape.
Rosie darted in, swinging her sword.
'You're down,' she yelled.

Lulu pretended to fall. She dropped to the ground and rolled over. Both dogs came to lick her back to life.

Mum came to the back door.
She smiled as she watched them play.
'Careful, you little warriors.'

Mum waved a piece of paper in the air. 'Lulu, can you please tell Gumpa that the tea is ready? And I've just checked the note from your teacher. It looks like we have a *huge* week coming up.'

Chapter 2

Feathered Friends

Everyone came up into the house.
Nanna was already sitting at the kitchen
table. The table was set with teacups and
a milk jug. Mum had made a pot of tea
for the adults. There was a fruit platter
for the kids.

'Check your weapons at the door,
honey buns,' joked Mum. 'No sword
fights in the kitchen.'

Lulu, Rosie and Gus propped up their swords in the corner. Mum poured out the tea for Nanna and Gumpa. Everyone sat around the table.

'So what did the note say?' asked Lulu. 'What exciting things are happening at school?'

Mum picked up her teacup and took a sip. 'It's Harmony Day next week,' said Mum. She turned to Nanna and Gumpa. 'I'm the class parent for year four. So it's my job to organise the food stall and the decorations.'

'Oooh,' said Rosie. 'I love Harmony Day.'

'It sounds like fun,' said Nanna, 'but what is Harmony Day?'

'Everyone dresses up in national costumes,' said Lulu. 'At lunchtime there's lots of yummy food from different countries. One of the classes is chosen to do a special performance.'

Mum put her teacup down in her saucer. 'It's a celebration of the many countries around the world where different families come from,' said Mum. 'Every class is allocated a culture based on the background of one of the kids in the class.'

'It's one of the best days of the year,' said Rosie. 'I think my class is celebrating India.'

'So will you wear a sari to school?' asked Nanna.

Rosie shook her head. 'The food and decorations will be Indian – and I *could* wear a sari – but most kids wear a costume that shows where their family came from,' she said.

'For our family that would be Scottish, Irish, Welsh, English, French and Spanish,' said Mum.

Gumpa laughed. 'Lots to choose from there. What country is your class celebrating, Lulu?'

'We don't know yet,' said Lulu. 'It won't be Holland because we did that last year.'

Last year, Jo and Olivia's dad had cooked *poffertjes*. These were puffy Dutch pancakes, served with sugar and butter. The year before it had been Sri Lanka and Lauren's dad had made egg hoppers and roti.

'It might be Vietnam this year,' said Mum. 'Tien could help us make lots of rice paper rolls.'

13

Gus nodded happily as he crunched his pear. *'Dulishus.* Gussie loves Tien rolls.'

Lulu's best friend Molly lived next door. Her mum Tien had originally come from Vietnam and she made the most wonderful Vietnamese food.

Suddenly there was a loud noise from outside. It was a cawing, squawking sound. Lulu jumped up and looked out the window.

'The cockies are here,' said Lulu. She ran to the pantry, grabbed a handful of sunflower seeds from a container, and slipped them into her pocket.

Outside were three sulphur-crested cockatoos perched on the branches of a tree. They raised their yellow crests and screamed in greeting.

Lulu stood out on the deck. She put a sunflower seed flat on the palm of her hand. Then she stretched her arm out wide.

'Cocky,' called Lulu. One of the cockatoos hopped from foot to foot. Then he spread his wings and flew towards Lulu. He landed on Lulu's arm. Gently he took the seed in his curved beak and crunched it.

Another cockatoo flew over and landed on Lulu's shoulder. He had a scarred foot with a missing toe. Lulu fed him a seed.

The rest of Lulu's family came to the door to watch. Mum closed the back door so the dogs wouldn't scare away the birds.

'Wow,' said Nanna. 'Lulu, you are amazing. You have wild cockatoos eating out of your hand!'

Lulu took the rest of the seeds and held them in the palm of her hand.

The third cockatoo joined the party.
He perched on the heel of Lulu's hand,
his head on one side, begging for a seed.
Lulu held her arms still so they could
peck up the rest of the seeds.

'They come to visit us most
afternoons,' said Lulu. 'They love eating
sunflower seeds or nuts. We've given
them all names. Let me introduce Rocky,
Cocky and Locky.'

Nanna laughed. 'And can you tell
them apart?'

Lulu nodded. 'Yes. Rocky is the oldest so he's looking a bit scarred. Cocky is the boldest and Locky is the handsomest.'

'Hello, Cocky,' yelled Gus. He stretched his arms wide and rushed forward. The cockatoos flew into the air with a screech. They wheeled up in the grey sky and flew away.

'Gus,' scolded Lulu with one hand on her hip. 'How many times have I told you not to frighten the birds?'

Chapter 3

The New Girl

On Tuesday morning, Lulu was at Shelly Beach School. Her new year four teacher Mr Newbold was sitting at his desk marking the roll.

There was a knock at the door. Mrs Poole from the office came in. Beside her was a girl with very long, straight, dark hair. Lulu thought she looked scared.

'Good morning, 4N,' said Mrs Poole. 'We have a student new to Shelly Beach School. Her name is Amira. I hope you all make her feel welcome.'

Mr Newbold stood up and smiled at her. Amira looked down at her toes.

'Welcome to 4N, Amira,' said Mr Newbold.

He turned to the class. 'Molly, would you mind moving to sit near Lauren?' he said. 'Amira, you can sit next to Lulu. She'll look after you and help you settle in.'

Molly gathered up her pencils and books. She moved to sit beside Lauren. Amira sat down beside Lulu.

'Hi, Amira,' said Lulu. 'My name is Lulu Bell.'

Amira whispered something as she unpacked her pencil case but Lulu didn't quite hear.

Mr Newbold walked back to his desk. 'As you all know, next Tuesday is Harmony Day.

'Today we find out what country our class will celebrate. And the principal has asked me if our class can do the special performance this year.'

A buzz of excitement rippled around the classroom.

'So we need to come up with a fantastic idea for the show,' said Mr Newbold. 'But first we need to do some work.'

'Oooh,' groaned the class.

The morning sped by as the class did reading in groups and then maths. Lulu loved maths. It was one of her favourite subjects.

After maths it was recess. Lulu and her friends went out to where their bags were hanging on hooks. Everyone was laughing and chatting as they found their hats and food. Amira looked around at the commotion.

Lulu took her apple out of her backpack. She turned to Amira and smiled.

'We usually play handball at recess,' said Lulu. 'Would you like to join us?'

'I need something from the office,' whispered Amira.

'Would you like me to take you?' asked Lulu.

Amira shook her head. 'I know where it is.'

'Come and find us afterwards,' said Lulu. 'We play on the handball courts near the front gate.'

Amira nodded.

Handball was the most popular playground game at Shelly Beach School. A big group of Lulu's friends played handball every day. There was Lulu, Molly, Lauren, Olivia, Jo, Max, Daniel, Zac and Flynn. There were several handball courts painted on the playground.

Lulu made it to king position before getting out. She laughed and skipped off the court. Lauren and Molly were practising next to the court, waiting their turn.

'Have you seen Amira?' asked Lulu.

'She doesn't know anyone. I hope she's not feeling left out.'

Lauren shook her head.

'I think I'll have a quick look for her,' said Lulu. 'She might be lost.'

Molly went with her. The girls searched the playground. They checked the office and the sick bay. Amira was nowhere to be found.

'Perhaps she's in the library?' suggested Molly.

The girls went inside. At first glance it seemed to be empty, but Lulu thought she heard a slight sound.

'Amira?' Lulu called softly. There was no reply. Lulu searched between the bookshelves. Amira was sitting on the floor with her arms wrapped around her knees. She looked utterly miserable.

'Are you all right, Amira?' asked Lulu.

Amira looked down at her school shoes. 'I'm okay,' she said.

'Why don't you come and play handball?' asked Molly.

Amira gave a watery smile. 'Thanks, but I don't really feel like it,' she said.

'Has someone upset you?' asked Lulu.

Amira shook her head. 'I'm just feeling a bit sad. It's all so strange being at a new school. I miss my old friends and my old house. And –'

Amira rubbed her eyes. Lulu held out her hand.

'Come on, Amira,' said Lulu. 'We need to think of ideas for Harmony Day next week. Why don't you come and help us?'

Chapter 4

Performance Preparations

 The bell rang and everyone hurried into class. Mr Newbold looked around. 'Now we'll have some fun getting ready for Harmony Day. I know you're all wondering what culture we'll be celebrating.'

Mr Newbold made a loud drumroll noise, banging his palms on the desk. 'The country for 4N this year will be ... Amira's homeland, Iran.'

Everyone turned to look at Amira. She flushed bright red and looked down at her hands in her lap.

'That's great, Amira,' whispered Lulu.

Amira nodded.

'Iran is a country in the Middle East that was once part of the vast Persian empire,' explained Mr Newbold. 'Most people in Iran speak Persian and much of their culture comes from its ancient traditions. It's a fascinating culture – so let's see what we can discover.'

The class was split up into five groups to research Persian food, music, dress, dance and history. Lulu was in a group with Amira, Molly, Max and Daniel.

After lunch, the students discussed ideas for the performance. They looked up photos and information on the class computers.

'It says here that wrestling and martial arts are traditional Iranian sports,' said Max. 'We could have a giant wrestling match.'

Max began tussling with Daniel. Daniel fell off his chair.

'Did you know the Persians invented polo?' added Daniel. He wiggled his eyebrows. 'Maybe we could play polo?'

Lulu giggled. 'You need to ride horses to play polo,' she said.

'It would be cool if we could ride camels,' said Max. 'Did you ride camels when you lived in Iran, Amira?'

Amira shook her head. 'I lived in a big city called Tehran. There were definitely no camels there.'

Daniel shrugged. 'That's a shame. We could have dressed up as camels.'

Lulu laughed and shook her head. The ideas seemed to be going from bad to worse. 'No camels! Our performance has to be something really special. All the parents are coming to watch it.'

Molly frowned. 'This is really hard.'

Just then the final bell rang. Lulu raced out into the playground. Mum was there, chatting to some of the other parents. Gus was climbing on the monkey bars with his friends. Lulu gave Mum a hug.

'So do we know the theme for our food stall yet?' asked Mum.

'Yes,' said Lulu. 'It's Iranian. We have
a new girl in our class called Amira, and
she's from Iran. She's over there.'

Lulu pointed. Amira was talking
to her mother. The two of them were
standing alone near the fence.

'Come on, honey bun,' said Mum.
'I think we should introduce ourselves.
I need to talk to Amira's mother about
some ideas for our feast.'

Mum and Lulu walked over to join
Amira and her mother.

'Hello,' said Mum. 'My name is
Chrissie Bell and this is my daughter
Lulu. She's in Amira's class.'

Amira's mother smiled. 'Nice to
meet you. My name is Leyla,' she said.

'I'm the class parent for 4N,'
explained Mum. 'Amira might have told
you that next week we are having a

32

special festivity. We're making an Iranian feast for all the children in the class.'

'Amira was just telling me,' Leyla said. 'That's lovely.'

Mum explained all about the plans for the day.

'I was hoping you might be able to help me choose the menu,' said Mum. 'Amira, perhaps you have some favourite dishes that you would like us to cook?'

Amira nodded. 'My mum cooks the best food. She makes *mezze* and *dolma* and *kabab*.'

'That sounds delicious,' said Mum. 'A few of the parents have offered to help make the meals. We just need some recipes and directions.'

'Amira and I would be happy to help,' said Leyla.

'Wonderful,' said Mum. 'Perhaps you'd like to come home with us after school tomorrow? We could talk about it over a cup of tea.'

Leyla beamed at Mum. 'That would be lovely. My husband has just started a new job so we only moved to Shelly Beach this week. We don't know anyone here yet.'

'You'll love it here,' said Lulu. 'Shelly Beach is the best.'

Chapter 5

Bird Rescue

At home that afternoon, Lulu sat at the
kitchen bench doing her homework.
She did her maths first. Then she sat and
looked at the photos of Iran that Mum
had helped her to find on the internet.
There were photos of domes and spires.
Of bustling markets and vast deserts. Of
musicians playing drums, tambourines,
stringed lutes and flutes. Of whirling
dancers in colourful robes.

Just then, Rosie and Gus came rushing in from the garden. They were fighting with swords, clashing the blades together with loud thwacks. Lulu covered her ears.

'Not so loud,' complained Lulu. 'I'm doing my homework.'

'Take that,' yelled Gus.

Rosie spun around, her cloak flying. She heaved her sword down upon Gus's blade.

'Be gone, foul knight,' she cried.

'No swords inside, honey buns,' called Mum as she came through the door. 'Sword fights are definitely an outside activity.'

Rosie and Gus galloped back outside but Rosie's twirl had reminded Lulu of something. What could it be?

Then Lulu had it. It was a drawing in the book *The Arabian Nights*, in the story

'Ali Baba and the Forty Thieves'. The drawing showed the slave girl Morgiana saving her master by fighting off the bandit captain.

Lulu rushed to her bedroom to find the book. She opened the book to the right page. There it was: a beautiful drawing of the slave girl dancing with a sword in her hand.

Lulu began to read the folktale again. Then she ran to the kitchen and started to jot down some ideas in her homework book.

Lulu had just finished when Dad popped his head around the green door that separated their home from the vet hospital in front.

'Where's my little bird whisperer?' asked Dad.

Lulu smiled up at him. 'Here I am, Dad.'

'Great, sweetie,' replied Dad. 'Are you ready to go on a bird rescue mission?'

Lulu jumped up. 'Of course I am.'

'Grab a pocketful of birdy treats and let's go.'

Lulu took a handful of seeds from the pantry and slipped them in her pocket.

It was nearly dusk. Lulu met Dad at the garage and they jumped in the car. Dad put a birdcage on the back seat next to her.

'Where are we heading, Dad?' asked Lulu, as she did up her seatbelt.

'To an apartment up on Tower Hill,' replied Dad. 'A man called Mr Capello rang. He said a bird has taken refuge on his balcony. It was being attacked by wild birds.'

'I wonder what sort of bird it is?' asked Lulu.

'We'll see if you can pick it,' said Dad.

The apartment building was high on the crest of the hill. Mr Capello lived up on the sixth floor. He answered the front door and led them through to the lounge room. Dad carried the birdcage.

'I hope it's still there,' said Mr Capello. 'It's an unusual looking bird that's been coming and going for a few days.'

'Have you tried to catch it?' asked Dad.

Mr Capello shook his head as he opened the sliding door onto the balcony.

'No. It seems frightened. I've called but it wouldn't come.'

Mr Capello, Dad and Lulu stood in the doorway and looked out.

The balcony had a stunning view over the town below, and out to the vast blue sea gleaming in the distance. Lulu could see the golden crescent of sand, the breaking surf and tiny people strolling along the walkway next to the beach. To the west the sun was setting in a blaze of reds, oranges and purples. She looked around the balcony. There was no sign of a bird.

Dad put the cage down on a table on the balcony. He pegged open the door to the cage. A large cob of corn was inside. 'We'll wait a while and see if it comes. Birds usually find a place to roost at sunset. Let's hope he comes back here.'

A few minutes later, Lulu spotted
a small parrot flying towards them.
'Look,' she cried. 'Is that it?'

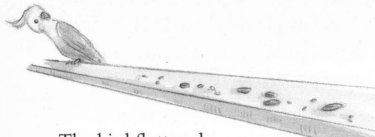

The bird fluttered
down and landed on the railing. Its body
was grey and white. It had a yellow crest
and neck and two orange spots on its
cheeks. It looked warily at the humans.

'A cockatiel,' whispered Lulu. The
bird flared its crest with alarm.

'That plumage shows he's a male,'
said Dad. 'He'll be missing his family.'

The bird hopped away from them,
further down the railing.

'Stay still, Mr Capello,' suggested
Dad. 'Lulu, see if you can tempt our little
feathered friend with some seeds.'

Lulu moved slowly and quietly. She
popped a seed onto the railing about two

metres away from the bird then stepped back. The bird watched her, its head cocked to the side. When Lulu moved away the cockatiel hopped towards the seed. It pecked up the food then hopped away.

Lulu repeated the process, placing the seed a little closer to the bird each time. Finally she placed the seed on her outstretched palm and offered it to the cockatiel. The bird watched Lulu warily, its head on its side. Lulu stayed perfectly still.

At last it hopped across onto Lulu's hand. It pecked up the sunflower seed. Lulu slowly put up her finger and pressed it gently against his chest. After a few seconds, the cockatiel perched on her outstretched finger. He fluffed up his feathers.

'Good work, sweetie,' whispered Dad. 'Now see if you can bring him towards the cage. Just slowly.'

Lulu crept forwards. She stretched out her hand towards the cage door. Just as Lulu was nearly there, the cockatiel stretched his wings and took flight. He flew straight from Lulu's hand to the open door of the cage. He perched for a moment on the threshold then hopped inside.

Dad released the peg to close the door. 'Great work, sweetie,' said Dad. The cockatiel nuzzled the corn then looked up at Lulu and whistled. 'We'll take him back to the vet hospital.'

'I hope you can track down his owner,' said Mr Capello.

'Don't worry,' said Lulu with confidence. 'We often find lost pets. And we nearly *always* find where they belong.'

Chapter 6

Arabian Nights

The next day was spent preparing for
the performance. The class broke up into
their groups. Lulu, Amira, Molly, Max
and Daniel discussed all their thoughts.
They decided to combine their best
ideas together.

Each group had a minute to outline
their plan to the class. Some of the
groups presented ideas about singing

songs, playing traditional musical
instruments and reciting poems.
Finally it was Lulu's group's turn.

Amira spoke first. She looked around
the classroom nervously. 'I came to
Australia from Iran when I was six years
old. The people who live in Iran are part
of a very ancient civilisation stretching
back nearly seven thousand years. Music
and dance have always been an important
part of our culture.'

Amira looked at Lulu. She was a
little nervous. 'I thought we could do a
traditional Persian dance,' she said. 'We
could also play drums and tambourines.

'But then Lulu had an idea, which
I really liked,' continued Amira. 'It was
to combine music and dancing with an
old Persian folktale.'

Amira nodded towards Lulu.

'Why don't you tell them about it, Lulu?'

Lulu smiled at Amira. She stepped forward.

'We thought we could act out a play,' suggested Lulu. 'At home we've been reading *The Arabian Nights.* There are some wonderful Persian folk stories including "Ali Baba and the Forty Thieves".'

Lulu held up the book she had brought to school and showed her class the illustrations.

'In the story, Ali Baba is a poor woodcutter,' said Lulu. 'One day, Ali Baba discovers a cave filled with wonderful treasure.

It's the hideout for a gang of forty thieves.
The entrance can only be revealed by
saying the magical words "open sesame".
There are lots of adventures when the
forty bandits try to find out who has
discovered their lair.'

Lulu jiggled on her toes.

'It's an exciting story, full of action,
twists and turns, and wicked villains.
Ali Baba and his family are saved by
a brave and clever slave girl called
Morgiana. She outwits the captain of
the thieves and reveals his identity.'

'There are lots of characters,' said
Amira. 'So everyone would have a
part to play.'

'Thanks, Amira and Lulu,' said
Mr Newbold. 'That sounds great. Now
it's time to vote on our favourite ideas.'

Mr Newbold asked everyone to write down which idea they liked best. All the slips of paper were put into a bucket then counted.

'Well done,' said Mr Newbold. 'Everyone had such great ideas. But it looks like Amira's group has come up with a winner. So a play it is!'

Lulu and Molly grinned at Amira with delight.

Mr Newbold looked around at all the kids. 'We need to get cracking! This afternoon we will allocate a role to everyone and start practising. We want this to be a fabulous performance.'

Lulu's mind started ticking over. *Who would play the main parts? What costumes would they need? Could they possibly get everything done in time?*

Chapter 7

Taj

That afternoon, Lulu and Amira ran
out together after school. Mum was
standing talking to Amira's mum in the
playground. Rosie and Gus were already
waiting, together with Amira's two
younger sisters, Zahra and Mina.

They all walked up the hill towards
home. Mum and Leyla sat at the kitchen
table, drinking tea. They talked about
different ideas for the feast.

Leyla wrote out the recipes of some of Amira's favourite dishes. Rosie played with Amira's sisters.

Lulu showed Amira around. She saw Lulu and Rosie's bedroom and met all the pets. There were Asha and Jessie, the family dogs. The two cats, Pepper and Pickles, were sleeping curled in the sun. In the garden was Flopsy, the bunny, and the ducklings. Mika the orphan wallaby was also staying with the Bells for a while.

Amira gave Flopsy a big cuddle. 'You're lucky to have so many pets,' said Amira. 'I don't have a pet. We did have one, but . . .' Amira looked sad.

Lulu felt sorry for Amira. It sounded like something bad had happened. She tried to think of something to cheer her up.

'Do you want to go next door to see our vet hospital?' asked Lulu. 'There's always something fun happening there.'

'I'd love to,' replied Amira.

Lulu led Amira through the green door that separated their house from the vet hospital. Lulu showed Amira the operating theatres, the hospital ward and the X-ray room. Then she led Amira into the reception. Kylie, the vet nurse, was weighing a golden retriever on the dog scales.

'Hello, girls,' called Kylie. 'Did you have a good day at school?'

'Hi, Kylie. It was great,' said Lulu. 'I'd like you to meet my friend Amira.'

Kylie and Amira said hello. Suddenly a loud chirping came from the corner.

Amira swung around. There in the corner of the waiting room was a tall, white birdcage. Inside was a smoky grey parrot with a yellow crest and orange cheeks.

'That's our mystery cockatiel,' said Lulu. 'We rescued him last night. But we haven't found his owner.'

Amira hurried to the cage. She pressed her face against the bars.

'Taj?' she cried. 'Is that you?'

The little bird chittered and chattered. He hopped over towards Amira and gently nibbled her finger through the bars. Amira began to cry.

'Oh, Taj,' said Amira. 'I thought I'd never see you again.'

Lulu looked at Amira in astonishment. 'Do you mean the cockatiel is yours?'

Amira nodded, beaming a huge smile through her tears.

'Yes,' said Amira. 'You see, I always used to let Taj fly free around our flat. But we moved to a new flat at Shelly Beach and he didn't know his way around.'

Amira opened the cage door a little and slipped her finger through the crack. The cockatiel hopped straight on her finger. He bent over and rubbed his beak against her hand.

'I didn't know that one of the windows was open,' said Amira. 'Taj flew around in confusion then escaped out the window. I was so worried.'

'Oh, no,' said Lulu. 'You must have been terrified.'

'I called and called his name,' explained Amira. 'I asked all our neighbours if they'd seen him. By night-time there was still no sign of him. Dad said he could have flown kilometres away by then, so I thought I would never see him again.'

Taj chirruped and put his head to one side. It was as though he knew they were talking about him.

'I'm so happy for you,' said Lulu. 'Isn't it lucky that you came over this afternoon?'

Amira took her finger out from the cage. Taj hopped onto his perch.

'I can't tell you how glad I am,' said Amira. 'Thanks, Lulu.'

'Come on,' said Lulu. 'Let's go and show Taj to your mum.'

Chapter 8

Ali Baba

The next few days were a blur of planning, preparing and rehearsing. There were costumes to organise, props to find and a set to create. The children practised the play over and over again until they remembered their lines. Mum and Leyla worked hard to help get everything ready.

At last it was Harmony Day.

Amira's mum had brought rugs, cushions and copper pots and platters to use as decorations. Mum had painted a backdrop on an old sheet. It showed palm trees, village houses and a thin crescent moon.

Best of all were the costumes. Mum had made a Persian-inspired costume for Lulu in gorgeous colours. It had lilac pants and a purple jerkin with gold trimming. Lulu stuck her wooden sword into the wide yellow sash around her waist.

Amira wore a long, flared dress with narrow trousers underneath. Her costume was hot pink and turquoise. Her dark hair hung loose to her waist and was covered by a floating veil and, on the top of her head, she wore a headdress of jangly silver coins. The other kids wore an assortment of bright tunics, veils and turbans.

After recess, the students of Shelly Beach School filed into the assembly hall. The kids sat cross-legged on the floor,

all wearing their national costumes.
Parents sat up the back on chairs.

The stage had been transformed into
an ancient Persian landscape. Lulu peeked
out onto the stage. She felt a thrill of
nerves. She hoped everyone would love
their performance.

Mr Newbold started the music player.
The hall filled with the striking sound of
Persian song.

Amira walked up and took her
place on the side of the stage. She was
the narrator.

'The students of 4N would like
to present the story of "Ali Baba and
the Forty Thieves", from *The Arabian
Nights*,' began Amira. 'This is a collection
of folktales from all over the Middle
East, but particularly from the ancient
empire of Persia. The Persian culture is

still celebrated by many people from my homeland of Iran.'

The audience clapped and cheered. Amira looked graceful and proud in her traditional costume.

'Once there lived a poor woodcutter called Ali Baba,' said Amira. Zac strolled onto the stage, dressed as Ali Baba. He was carrying a pile of sticks.

'He lived with his wife and son in a small town. While Ali Baba was very poor, his brother Cassim had a rich wife. Cassim lived next door to Ali Baba.

'One day Ali Baba was collecting firewood in the forest when he heard a terrible commotion,' continued Amira. 'Fearing for his life, Ali Baba hid so he was out of sight. It was lucky he did, because a gang of forty ferocious thieves appeared.'

Lively music began. A swarm of kids ran onto the stage. Some of the children held drums or tambourines. They stood at the back and began playing their instruments. Some of children were carrying bulging sacks. They dropped their sacks in a large pile and began a dance. They twirled and jumped and kicked, circling their swords high in the air. The dance finished with a fierce yell from all the children.

Daniel, dressed as the captain of the thieves, swaggered up to a large rock on the side of the stage. 'Open sesame,' he bellowed.

The rock slid aside to reveal a dark space.

'Behold our treasure cave,' said Daniel. 'We have gold and silver, rubies and emeralds. We'll hide them here and be rich forever.'

'Hooray!' yelled the children. They stuffed the sacks into the cave. When all the treasure was safely stowed, Daniel stood in front of the cave.

'Close sesame,' he roared. The rock slid back across the cave entrance and the children ran off the stage, brandishing their weapons.

Zac crept out from his hiding spot. He came to the front of the rock. 'Open sesame,' he cried.

The rock slid open. Zac fell to his knees. He pulled a sack from the cave. Treasure, coins and jewels spilled from the bag.

'I'm rich!' cried Zac. 'I'm rich!'

Chapter 9

Morgiana

Amira spread her arms wide. 'Ali Baba ran all the way home, carrying a bag of treasure. He was greeted at home by his wife.'

Molly was acting in the part of Ali Baba's wife. Molly and Zac danced together with excitement as they examined the coins.

'I'll bury the treasure so no-one can find it,' said Zac.

'Yes, but first we should weigh it,' said Molly. 'There's far too much to count. I'll go next door and borrow a set of scales from your brother Cassim.'

Amira continued to narrate the story. 'Cassim's wife was suspicious and placed some wax at the bottom of the scales. When the scales were returned she discovered that a gold coin had stuck to the wax. She showed her husband, who insisted that his brother Ali Baba tell him where he had found such fabulous treasure.'

Amira gestured towards the rock on the side of the stage. Max, who was playing the part of greedy Cassim, marched up to the rock and yelled, 'Open sesame.' The rock rolled aside and Max crawled inside.

'Cassim went inside the magical cave,'

continued Amira. 'He shouted "close sesame" to shut the door. But he was so excited by all the treasure inside that he forgot the magic words to open the door again. Cassim was trapped inside.'

The opening to the cave closed, hiding Max. But just as it closed, kids dressed as thieves rushed onto the stage, waving their swords. The captain stood before the rock and yelled, 'Open sesame.'

Amira pointed to the thieves. 'The forty bandits discovered Cassim stealing their treasure. They dragged him from the cave and made him confess how he had learnt its secret.'

'It was my brother Ali Baba who discovered your secret,' Max cried.

'We must find Ali Baba before he can tell anyone else about our treasure,' said Daniel, captain of the thieves.

All the children ran off the stage, pushing the rock with them.

'Luckily for Ali Baba, he had a clever and brave slave girl called Morgiana,' said Amira.

Lulu came onto the stage carrying a basket on her head. She was dressed as Morgiana the slave girl. Lulu sat cross-legged on the ground and began to

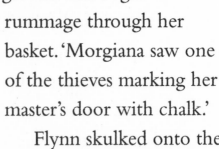

rummage through her basket. 'Morgiana saw one of the thieves marking her master's door with chalk.'

Flynn skulked onto the stage, looking suspicious. He drew a chalk mark onto one of the houses painted on the backdrop. Lulu watched him, pretending she was busy with her basket. Flynn looked around then slipped away.

'Morgiana guessed that the captain of the thieves would be back later to find her master. As soon as the thief had left, Morgiana marked all the neighbourhood doors with chalk so that the captain wouldn't know which one was her master's,' explained Amira.

Lulu put her basket down and ran around, drawing white chalk marks on the other houses.

'The robber captain was furious to find his plot had been foiled,' continued Amira. 'Finally he discovered which house belonged to Ali Baba. He disguised himself as an oil merchant. Then he hid the thirty-nine other thieves inside oil jars. He planned to have the thieves capture Ali Baba in the middle of the night.'

Daniel came on stage, wearing
a turban and a long cape. The other
children followed him. Each one carried
a piece of cardboard cut into the shape of
an oil jar. They crouched down behind
their jars.

'The captain knocked on Ali
Baba's door and said that he was an
oil merchant on his way to the market
but had nowhere to stay the night. Ali
Baba welcomed him and Morgiana was

ordered to prepare a bed and cook a feast for the stranger.

'But when Morgiana went into the courtyard to get some oil from one of the jars, she discovered what was really inside. Thirty-nine thieves!'

Lulu pulled away a cardboard jar to reveal one of the children hiding there. Lulu shook the jar and the thief ran away squealing. Lulu chased all of the thieves off the stage. The audience roared with laughter.

Daniel, Zac and Molly came onstage and sat on a pile of cushions. Lulu came onstage carrying a tray of silver goblets which she served to the others.

Lulu curtseyed and pulled her sword from her sash. 'Master, may I dance for you?' she asked. 'I would like to honour our guest with an ancient Persian sword dance.'

'Of course, Morgiana,' said Zac.

Persian music began to play. Lulu danced, holding the sword above her head with two hands. She swayed and spun and turned cartwheels. Lulu swished the sword in the air, making circles and figure-eights. Lulu danced closer and closer to the group seated on the cushions.

Suddenly, Lulu lunged with her sword and pointed it at Daniel.

'Morgiana, what are you doing?' cried Zac. 'Release our guest at once.'

Lulu knocked off Daniel's turban with her sword. 'Look, master,' she said. 'He's not an oil merchant at all. He's the captain of the forty thieves and has come to attack us.'

Everyone onstage froze. Amira stepped forward to the middle of the stage.

'So Morgiana, the brave and clever slave girl, saved Ali Baba from the robber captain. Ali Baba was so happy that he set her free. Morgiana married Ali Baba's son and they were happy and wealthy for the rest of their days.'

All the children ran to the front of the stage. They bowed low. The audience clapped and clapped.

Amira and Lulu grinned at each other. Lulu stuck her sword back in her sash. *That was so much fun*, thought Lulu, bubbling with excitement. *And* everyone *loved it!*

Chapter 10

The Feast

 After the play, it was time for the feast.
The playground was filled with children
dressed in various costumes. Food stalls
were decorated with bunting, flags,
balloons and streamers. The Iranian stall
had giant cardboard palm trees. Gus,
dressed in his knight suit, was running
through the crowd.

Mum and Leyla were dressed in long
loose dresses, with scarves tied over their hair.

They served food to the kids. There were bowls of dates, apricots, peaches and grapes. A platter held *mezze*, with little dishes of olives, hummus dip, eggplant dip, and stuffed vine leaves called *dolma*. There was also flat *naan* bread. Large platters held barbecued lamb *kababs* with yoghurt sauce.

The children queued up with their plates and forks. Amira explained to Lulu and Molly what all the different dishes were.

'Try the *dolma*,' said Amira. '*Dolma* are vine leaves stuffed with meat and rice.'

Mum piled the girls' plates high with food. 'Amira, you were *wonderful* as the narrator,' she said.

Amira beamed a dazzling smile. 'Thanks. Everyone was great.'

Leyla gestured around at the playground buzzing with kids and parents. 'This is wonderful. I can't believe how welcome you've made us feel.'

Mum laughed. 'I'm so glad. Harmony Day is a fabulous celebration.'

The girls moved away so that the next children could be served.

'This is delicious,' said Lulu. 'I love the *mezze* and the *kababs*.'

Amira smiled. 'I'm glad you like it.'

Molly looked at Amira. 'It's lovely to see you smile.'

Amira gave Lulu and Molly a hug. 'When I started school last week I was so upset,' said Amira. 'I didn't want to move house. I didn't want to change schools. And I'd lost Taj. But you have both been so kind.'

Molly and Lulu hugged her back.
'We're just glad that you're happy again,'
said Lulu.

'There's just one thing,' said Amira.

'What's that?' asked Molly.

'Could you teach me how to play
handball?' asked Amira.

Illustrated by Serena Geddes

BELINDA
MURRELL

Lulu
Bell
and the
Koala Joey

Lulu Bell and the Koala Joey

Lulu can't wait for her holiday at Tarni Beach to begin. She has a new pink surfboard and Dad is going to teach her to surf.

Lulu and her friend Zac like to spot wildlife in the bush nearby. But what has happened to the mummy koala and her joey? Bulldozers have arrived and the trees might soon be gone. Lulu needs to work out how to save the koalas' home!

Out now

Read all the Lulu Bell books

Lulu Bell and the Birthday Unicorn

Lulu Bell and the Fairy Penguin

Lulu Bell and the Cubby Fort

Lulu Bell and the Moon Dragon

Lulu Bell and the Circus Pup

Lulu Bell and the Sea Turtle

Lulu Bell and the Tiger Cub

Lulu Bell and the Pyjama Party

Lulu Bell and the Christmas Elf

Lulu Bell and the Koala Joey

Lulu Bell and the Arabian Nights

Plus more to come!

About the Author

Belinda Murrell grew up in a vet hospital and Lulu Bell is based on some of the adventures she shared with her own animals. After studying Literature at Macquarie University, Belinda worked as a travel journalist, editor and technical writer.

A few years ago, she began to write stories for her own three children – Nick, Emily and Lachlan. Belinda's books include the Sun Sword fantasy trilogy and her children's novels *The Locket of Dreams*, *The Ruby Talisman*, *The Ivory Rose*, *The Forgotten Pearl*, *The River Charm* and *The Sequin Star*.

www.belindamurrell.com.au

About the Illustrator

Serena Geddes spent six years working with a fabulously mad group of talented artists at Walt Disney Studios in Sydney before embarking on the path of picture book illustration in 2009. She works both traditionally and digitally and has illustrated many books, ranging from picture books to board books to junior novels.

www.serenageddes.com.au